# The
# First Strawberries
## A · C H E R O K E E · S T O R Y

retold by **Joseph Bruchac**

pictures by **Anna Vojtech**

*Dial Books for Young Readers*  *New York*

## AUTHOR'S NOTE

Although I recall first hearing this story over a decade ago
(while talking with Mary and Goingback Chiltoskey,
Cherokee elders from North Carolina), the legend of the origin
of the first strawberries has been put down on paper
numerous times since it was first recorded in James Mooney's
*Myths of the Cherokee* (1900). More recently, Cherokee storytellers
Jean Starr, Gayle Ross, and Lloyd Arneach
helped me understand the story well enough to tell it.
—J.B.

Published by Dial Books for Young Readers
A member of Penguin Putnam Inc.
375 Hudson Street
New York, New York 10014

Text copyright © 1993 by Joseph Bruchac
Pictures copyright © 1993 by Anna Vojtech
All rights reserved
Design by Amelia Lau Carling
Printed in Hong Kong
by South China Printing Company (1988) Limited
First Edition
9  10

Library of Congress Cataloging in Publication Data
Bruchac, Joseph, 1942–
The first strawberries : a Cherokee story /
retold by Joseph Bruchac ; pictures by Anna Vojtech.—1st ed.
p.  cm.
Summary: A quarrel between the first man and the
first woman is reconciled when the Sun causes
strawberries to grow out of the earth.
ISBN 0-8037-1331-2.—ISBN 0-8037-1332-0 (lib.)
1. Cherokee Indians—Legends. [1. Cherokee
Indians—Legends. 2. Indians of North America—Legends.
3. Strawberries—Folklore.] I. Vojtech, Anna, ill. II. Title.
E99.C5B885  1993  398.2'089975—dc20  91-31058  CIP  AC

*The full-color artwork was prepared using watercolors and colored pencils.*

*For my Tsalagi friends*
*and teachers—Wado!*
J.B.

*To Roland*
A.V.

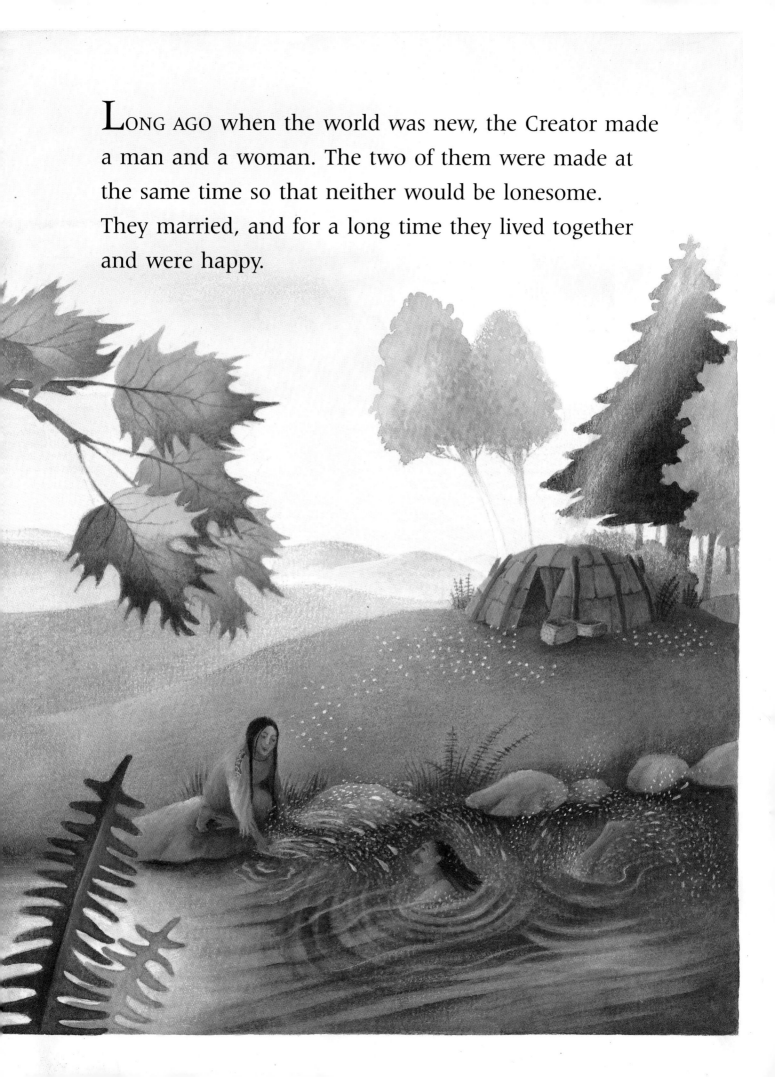

LONG AGO when the world was new, the Creator made a man and a woman. The two of them were made at the same time so that neither would be lonesome. They married, and for a long time they lived together and were happy.

Then one afternoon the man came home from hunting and found that the woman had not yet begun to prepare their meal. Instead she was out picking flowers.

The man grew angry.

"I am hungry," he said in a cold voice. "Do you expect me to eat flowers?"

Now the wife, too, became angry. She had picked those flowers to share their beauty with her husband. "Your words hurt me," she said. "I will live with you no longer."

She turned to the west and began to walk toward the Sun. Her husband followed, but her steps were too quick. He could not catch her. He called her name, but she could not hear him. He went as fast as he could go, but his wife was much faster.

The Sun watched as the husband followed her. The Sun saw how sorry the man was and took pity on him.

"Are you still angry with your wife?" asked the Sun.

"No," said the man, "I was foolish to speak angry words. But I cannot catch her to tell her I am sorry."

"Then I will help you," said the Sun.

The Sun shone its light down on the Earth, in front of the woman. Where its light shone, raspberries grew up. The berries were ripe and looked good to eat, but the woman paid no attention to them and continued walking.

The Sun tried again. It shone down and blueberries grew. They glistened brightly in the sunlight, but the woman paid no attention to them. She only walked on toward the west, leaving her husband farther behind.

Now the Sun tried a third time. Where its beams touched the Earth, blackberries grew up. They were dark and plump, but the woman's anger was too great and she did not see them.

At last the Sun tried its hardest. It shone its light down in the grass right in front of the woman's feet, and strawberries appeared. They glowed like fire in the grass, and the woman had to stop when she saw them in front of her.

She knelt down and plucked one and bit into it. She had never tasted anything like it before. Its sweetness reminded her of how happy she and her husband had been together before they quarreled.

"I must gather some of this fruit for my husband," she said, and she began to pick the berries.

She was still picking them when the man caught up
to her.

"Forgive me for my hard words," he said to her. And she answered him by sharing the sweetness of the strawberries.

So it was that strawberries came into the world.

To this day, when the Cherokee people eat strawberries, they are reminded to always be kind to each other; to remember that friendship and respect are as sweet as the taste of ripe, red berries.